Sonali Gupta

The Curious Case of Neerja

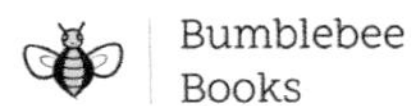

Bumblebee
Books

BUMBLEBEE PAPERBACK EDITION

A CIP catalogue record for this title is
available from the British Library.

ISBN: 978-1-83934-945-4

Bumblebee Books is an imprint of
Olympia Publishers.

First Published in 2024

Olympia Publishers
Tallis House
2 Tallis Street
London
EC4Y 0AB

Printed in Great Britain

Dedication

To my kids – Bhoomika and Siddharth

Ding dong, clang clang! The alarm rang as the dream of pitthu, an Indian game of marbles, faded away. Neerja stirred and stretched as the sound of the ball hitting the stack of marbles was replaced by her shrill alarm. Her mom had entered her room as Neerja was rubbing her eyes.

"Neeru, wakey-wakey!" chimed her mom. "It is time to rise and shine, baby!"

Neerja sighed and yawned while dragging herself to the bathroom. She wondered why her mom was always so chirpy in the mornings while she was always cranky.

Her mom, as usual, left her bedroom door open and now she could hear the morning commotion in the Gupta household. Her parents' ginger chai was brewing in the kitchen, Alexa was playing morning chants and her younger brother Roshan was bawling – his favourite activity – in his highchair while her father was busy making breakfast.

While brushing her teeth, she smiled, thinking about her dream. Moments ago, she was back home in sunny India, playing pitthu with her friends in her large back yard and now the sounds of the game were replaced by the sound of the cold wind whipping through the trees in America.

Let's rewind...

Neerja lived in New Delhi, India, for the ten years she had been on this planet. She was a bright and curious student who had many friends. She loved animals, especially dogs. Their family had two German shepherds, one corgi and a mutt they had rescued. She was good at everything: academics, sports and was learning Bharatnatyam – Indian classical dance. One thing she was not good at was public speaking. Her best friend Kavita was super confident and great at debates and public speaking; Neerja truly admired her for that. While Kavita was an obedient girl, Neerja was feisty and didn't like when others told her what to do, especially random aunties – her mom's friends – who would comment on her hair, clothes and grades. She secretly wished a bird would poop on their heads.

She lived in a beautiful apartment with her grandparents. She neither liked nor disliked her school, it all depended on what kind of friends she had. Thankfully, she had many friends from different parts of India who had moved to New Delhi.

She always said, "Not to flex, but I am very popular!" She was right. Neerja was social and extremely outgoing. She spoke Hindi and English with equal ease.

One day, her mom came back from work and said that they have to move to America. Although Neerja had travelled to New York and Los Angeles multiple times during her summer breaks, but she had never imagined going to school there. She was mortified. She secretly hated her mom for uprooting her. She thought to herself, *It sucks to be ten. If only I could make my own decisions!*

The worst part was they had to leave the dogs with her grandparents. Now let's go back to Neerja waking up from her dream...

It was the day of Diwali, and she had to go to school. How could that be? Why was it not a holiday in America? She got even more mad and cranky.

It had been four months since their move, but she couldn't help but feel homesick during this festive season. Last night when she was on FaceTime with Kavita, she felt a sense of envy at how Kavita was distracted because her house was full of her cousins, and they were all celebrating Choti Diwali – the day before the main Diwali day. Her house, on the other hand, was completely silent because Roshan had a pacifier in his mouth. Thank God her ears were spared!

Two months ago, she was really anxious to start school in a foreign land, but her school was really nice and welcoming. Her Grade 5 teacher Ms Abbot was kind and considerate. Her classmates were friendly and funny; it made her feel less like an outsider. She already had a close friend, not a best friend yet. No one could replace Kavita. Her close friend was Mateo. His parents had moved from Colombia. Neerja and her family were invited to his sister's quinceañera last month. Neerja was fascinated by the amazing tradition.

One of the things Neerja missed the most was celebrating Diwali – the festival of lights – with her family back in New Delhi. She missed the warm hugs from her grandparents, the colourful rangolis on the floor, the delicious sweets and savoury snacks, and the joyful prayers and rituals. She loved bursting crackers with her cousins.

So, Neerja went to school all grumpy on Diwali day.

As Neerja walked into the classroom, she was greeted by the sight of Ms Abbot wearing a bright red sari and a bindi on her forehead. Neerja's eyes lit up as she realised that Ms Abbot had dressed up for the occasion.

SCHOOL

"Happy Diwali, Neerja!" Ms Abbot exclaimed, giving her a warm hug.

Neerja's mood immediately brightened at the kind gesture. "Thank you, Ms Abbot. I can't believe you remembered!"

"Of course, I did," Ms Abbot replied. "I always make an effort to recognise and celebrate the cultural traditions of my students. And besides, who wouldn't want an excuse to wear a beautiful sari like this?"

As the day went on, Neerja found herself feeling less homesick and more grateful for the small ways in which her school and community were trying to include and celebrate her culture. She even invited Mateo over for dinner that evening to share some of the traditional Diwali treats her mom had prepared. It may not have been exactly the same as celebrating in India but Neerja realised that with a little effort and understanding, she could make new traditions and memories in her new home.

Neerja noticed that while most people vaguely knew about Diwali as the festival of lights, she knew it to be much deeper than that – thanks to all the knowledge shared by her grandmom. As a result, she decided to educate everyone in her class, as well as the rest of the school, about it.

However, how would she present to the whole school? She needed Kavita to encourage and support her. She missed her best friend even more.

At lunch Mateo sat next to her and said, "Hey Neerja, why do you seem so worried? Is everything okay?"

Neerja sighed and explained her dilemma to Mateo. "I really want to share the true meaning of Diwali with everyone in our school, but I'm not sure how to go about it. I don't want to just stand in front of the whole school and lecture them, but I also want to make sure I do justice to the significance of the festival."

Mateo nodded understandingly. "I see what you mean. Have you thought about doing a presentation or putting together some kind of activity or workshop for the students? That way, it's not just a one-way conversation, and everyone can participate and learn more actively."

Neerja brightened at the suggestion. "That's a great idea, Mateo! I could create a presentation with some information about the history and significance of Diwali, and then maybe we can make a rangoli as an interactive activity. What do you think?"

"What is a rangoli?" Mateo questioned. Neerja excitedly told him to be patient and wait for the presentation.

"I think that sounds like a great plan," Mateo replied with a smile. "And why don't you add a Kahoot or a Blooket quiz at the end? I'm happy to lend a hand."

Neerja thanked Mateo and began to feel more confident about her idea. She knew that with a little creativity and teamwork, she

could educate her schoolmates about the true meaning of Diwali and help them appreciate the richness and the depth of the festival.

Neerja's mind started running in all directions at the prospect. She hugged Mateo and sprinted out of the cafeteria, saying, "You will love making a rangoli, Mateo!"

The next day, Neerja approached Ms Abbott first and then the head of school – Ms Choi – and asked if she could give a presentation about Diwali to the whole school. Ms Choi was happy to oblige, and Neerja was over the moon.

She ran to her room after school, gathered pictures and videos of Diwali celebrations in India and printed out some informational sheets about the history and significance of the holiday. Since her mother was travelling for work, Neerja helped her father make delicious Diwali treats at home to share with her classmates.

She wore her favourite lehenga-choli – long skirt with a top – along with bindi on her forehead and bangles on her wrists.

She wanted to make her parents and her grandparents proud. A small part of her even wanted to make little Roshan proud of his elder sister, although she always considered him to be an annoying toad.

Ms Choi, the head of school, conducted the assembly every Friday; she was really funny. She would start by playfully roasting teachers and students and then move on to important announcements and updates. The students loved Ms Choi's assemblies because they were always entertaining and informative.

She talked about upcoming events, such as the school's talent show and the sports teams' schedules. She also reminded the students to turn in their permission slips for the field trip to the museum next week.

After the announcements, Ms Choi introduced the guest speaker for the day: a local firefighter who talked to the students about fire safety and the importance of having a plan in case of an emergency. The students listened attentively and asked the firefighter questions about his job and what to do in case of a fire.

She then introduced Neerja on to the stage for a 'special' presentation.

As Neerja reached for the mike on the podium, her hands shook as she clutched the papers containing her Diwali presentation. Standing up in front of all those people made her stomach churn.

As she took her place at the front of the room, Neerja's heart pounded in her chest. She could feel the sweat starting to bead on her forehead, and her mouth had gone completely dry. She tried to take a deep breath to calm her nerves but it only made her feel more lightheaded.

Despite her fear, Neerja forced herself to screen share from her iPad to the projector and begin speaking. Her voice shook at first, but as she got into the content of her presentation, she began to feel more confident. She focused on the information she was sharing and tried to ignore the butterflies in her stomach.

She began her presentation with videos and photo collage of her family celebrating Diwali.

She mustered all the courage and began, "Diwali is a Hindu festival that celebrates the victory of good over evil and the return of Lord Rama, Sita and Lakshmana to Ayodhya after fourteen years

SCHOOL

of exile. It is also a time for people to come together with their families and friends, exchange gifts, participate in various rituals and traditions such as lighting diyas – oil lamps, setting off fireworks and decorating homes with rangoli designs."

Neerja explained to her classmates how the first day of Diwali, known as Dhanteras, is a day to worship the Hindu god of wealth, Kubera. She also told them about the tradition of buying new things, such as gold or silver, to bring good luck for the coming year.

Neerja then shared the story of how on the second day – known as Narak Chaturdashi – the god Vishnu killed the demon Narakasura to save the world from evil. She also told her classmates about the tradition of taking baths early in the morning and applying oil to the skin as a way to cleanse the body and mind.

Neerja described how people on the third day, known as Diwali or the Festival of Lights, decorate their homes with diyas – small clay lamps – and colourful rangolis – patterns made with rice flour or coloured sand. She also told them about the tradition of lighting fireworks and exchanging gifts with loved ones.

Neerja explained how the fourth day, known as Govardhan Puja, is dedicated to the worship of the god Krishna and the mountain Govardhan, which he lifted to protect his village from a destructive storm. She also told her classmates about the tradition of making and eating special dishes, such as puri and kachori.

Neerja described how the fifth and final day, known as Bhai

Dooj, is dedicated to the bond between brothers and sisters. She told her classmates about the tradition of sisters putting tilak – a sacred mark – on their brothers' foreheads and brothers giving gifts to their sisters as a sign of love and protection.

As the presentation came to a close, Neerja opened up the forum for a Q&A session. Mateo took the mike and asked, "Will you please tell us the importance of the rangoli art?"

Neerja felt guilty for forgetting to add that important piece of information to the slide show. However, she was thankful to Mateo for bringing it up.

Neerja looked at her notes and said, "Rangoli is a traditional art form that is practiced in India and other parts of South Asia during festivals and other special occasions. The word 'rangoli' comes from the Sanskrit word 'rangavalli', which means 'a row of colours'. It is a decorative design that is created using coloured powders, flowers, and other materials, and is usually drawn on the floor or ground in the front of homes and other buildings.

"During the festival of Diwali, rangoli is used as a way to decorate homes and public spaces and to welcome the goddess Lakshmi, who is believed to bring prosperity and good fortune. The patterns and designs of rangoli are typically inspired by nature, and they are believed to bring good luck and positive energy to the home."

She added, "Do pop into my class after school and I will be

happy to share some samples of rangolis and you can even try to make one yourself."

Then the mike was passed to Lisa from her class who asked about the reason behind fireworks. "Is there a historical significance or do children do it for fun?"

Neerja had learned so much through her research, she confidently started reading the points from her notes, "Fireworks are a significant part of the celebration of Diwali. In Hindu mythology, the festival of Diwali marks the victory of good over evil, light over darkness, and knowledge over ignorance. The use of fireworks is believed to help drive away evil spirits and bring good luck for the coming year.

"During Diwali, people light small clay lamps, or diyas, and place them around their homes and temples. Fireworks are also set off to add to the celebratory atmosphere. The use of fireworks during Diwali dates back to ancient times, when they were used to celebrate the victory of the Hindu god Rama over the demon king Ravana.

"In modern times, Diwali celebrations often include fireworks displays and the lighting of firecrackers. In some parts of India, it is traditional for families to set off fireworks in their own homes or in community areas. The use of fireworks during Diwali is a way to honour the gods and bring joy and celebration to the holiday."

Neerja couldn't help but feel a sense of accomplishment. Despite her initial nervousness about public speaking, she had managed to deliver a successful presentation. As she returned to her seat, she let out a sigh of relief, proud of herself for overcoming her stage fright. The Kahoot quiz suggested by Mateo was a hit with the students, who cheered and clapped as they competed to answer the questions. Neerja couldn't help but smile, thinking to herself that a little bit of friendly competition never hurt anyone. She knew she couldn't have done it without her new BEST FRIEND!

Neerja returned to the stage and picked up the microphone. "I want to give a huge thank you to Mateo for his support and encouragement in putting together this Diwali presentation," she said. "Without his help, I'm not sure I would have had the confidence to do it."

Mateo, who had turned a shade of red, was the centre of attention as everyone cheered.

Neerja's presentation was a success, and her classmates were grateful to learn about the rich history and traditions of Diwali. They even asked if they could celebrate the holiday with her next year. Neerja was thrilled and couldn't wait to share the joy of Diwali with her friends. Due to the environmental concerns and rising levels of pollution, she and her friends were mindful of not overdoing it.

When she was back in her classroom, her classmates asked lots of questions, and Neerja could see their faces lighting up with curiosity and understanding. She even brought out the sweets and treats she had made with her father, and they eagerly tried them, savouring the flavours and textures.

Everyone spent one whole lesson decorating the class with colourful rangolis. Ms Abbott joined the fun with equal enthusiasm.

Ms Choi suggested she and Mateo start a club that would help students participate and learn about the significance of different traditions and festivals. Neerja and Mateo decided to call it Culturama.

Like everyone else, Neerja was aware of Christmas and Eid, but she wanted to go further and discover with everyone the crucial facets of Hanukkah, Navroz, Eid, Christmas, and many more important festivities. She also wanted to encourage students to interact with the custom and culture.

As Neerja left the school that day, she couldn't help but feel grateful for the opportunity to celebrate Diwali in a new way, and to share the joy and beauty of her culture with others. And she knew that no matter where she was, the light of Diwali would always burn bright within her heart.

HAPPY DIWALI
FESTIVAL OF LIGHTS

About the Author

Meet Sonali Gupta, a dedicated mom, wife, and enthusiastic educator with a passion for yoga and healthy living. With a background in the airline industry and a love for travel, Sonali grew up in New Delhi, India, and has lived in various cities, including Mumbai, KL, Jakarta, and Dubai. After teaching Grade 5 for several years, Sonali now serves as an IB PYP Coordinator in an international school in Dubai. She brings a wealth of experience working with children from diverse backgrounds, including her own third culture kids. Recently, Sonali and her family welcomed Phoebe, a rescue Golden Retriever, into their home. When she's not coordinating PYP initiatives, Sonali enjoys spending quality time with her family and managing her beloved Golden Retriever Joey's social media account.

Acknowledgements

Thank you to my beautiful kids – Bhoomika and Siddharth, my husband Naveen and Aai.